GRANDPA AND ME ON TU B'SHEVAT

Marji E. Gold-Vukson Illustrations by Leslie Evans

KAR-BEN
PUBLISHING

Kar-Ben Publishing, Inc.
A division of Lerner Publishing Group
241 First Avenue North
Minneapolis, MN 55401 U.S.A.
800-4KARBEN

Website address: www.karben.com

Library of Congress Cataloging-in-Publication Data

Gold-Vukson, Marji E.
        Grandpa and me on Tu B'Shevat / Marji E. Gold-Vukson ; illustrations by Leslie Evans.
            p.   cm.
        Summary: In rhyming, cumulative verse, portrays the tradition of planting a tree on the holiday of Tu B'Shevat. Includes a list of ten ways to celebrate Tu B'Shevat.
        ISBN: 1-58013-122-0 (pbk. : alk. paper)
        [1. Tu B'Shevat—Fiction. 2. Trees—Planting—Fiction. 3. Grandfathers—Fiction. 4. Stories in rhyme.]
        I. Evans, Leslie, ill. II. Title.
        PZ8.3.G56450Gr 2004
        [E]—dc22   2003026459

Manufactured in the United States of America
1 2 3 4 5 6 - JR - 09 08 07 06 05 04

About Tu B'Shevat

Tu B'Shevat (the 15th of the Hebrew month of Shevat) is the Birthday of the Trees. The holiday falls in January or February, where in many parts of the world it is still winter. In Israel, however, the almond tree is beginning to bloom and is the first sign of spring. It is traditional to plant new trees on Tu B'Shevat. In places where it is too cold to plant, people celebrate with fruit-tasting parties. They sample the crops of Israel such as almonds, oranges, figs, dates, olives, and carob. Tu B'Shevat reminds us to care for trees and to use and recycle their products wisely.

To the memory of
Grandpa Marvin Gold (z"l)
and to Noah Ephraim,
his first grandchild
(and my inspiration).
—M. G. V.

To Miriam Mufson,
who delighted in sharing
her love of gardening
with her grandchildren.
—L. E.

This is the shovel, shiny and new, that Grandpa and I used on Tu B'Shevat.

This is the grass, 'neath a blanket of dew,
that was cleared with the shovel, shiny and new,
by Grandpa and me on Tu B'Shevat.

This is the hole (but that you knew!)
that we dug in the grass, 'neath a blanket of dew,
that was cleared with the shovel, shiny and new,
by Grandpa and me on Tu B'Shevat.

This is the peat, a warm, mulchy stew,
that lined the hole (but that you knew!)
that we dug in the grass, 'neath a blanket of dew,
that was cleared with the shovel, shiny and new,
by Grandpa and me on Tu B'Shevat.

This is the seed with a green curlicue,
tucked into the peat, a warm, mulchy stew,
that lined the hole (but that you knew!)
that we dug in the grass, 'neath a blanket of dew,
that was cleared with the shovel, shiny and new,
by Grandpa and me on Tu B'Shevat.

This is the soil, rich through and through,
that covered the seed with a green curlicue,
tucked into the peat, a warm, mulchy stew,
that lined the hole (but that you knew!)
that we dug in the grass, 'neath a blanket of dew,
that was cleared with the shovel, shiny and new,
by Grandpa and me on Tu B'Shevat.

This is the water, splish-splashy and blue,
that moistened the soil, rich through and through,
that covered the seed with a green curlicue,
tucked into the peat, a warm, mulchy stew,
that lined the hole (but that you knew!)
that we dug in the grass, 'neath a blanket of dew,
that was cleared with the shovel, shiny and new,
by Grandpa and me on Tu B'Shevat.

This is the sapling (from the small seed it grew!)
that drank up the water, splish-splashy and blue,
that moistened the soil, rich through and through,
that covered the seed with a green curlicue,
tucked into the peat, a warm, mulchy stew,
that lined the hole (but that you knew!)
that we dug in the grass, 'neath a blanket of dew,
that was cleared with the shovel, shiny and new,
by Grandpa and me on Tu B'Shevat.

This is the tree (and the tree's feathered crew)
that once was a sapling (from the small seed it grew!)
that drank up the water, splish-splashy and blue,
that moistened the soil, rich through and through,
that covered the seed with a green curlicue,
tucked into the peat, a warm, mulchy stew,
that lined the hole (but that you knew!)
that we dug in the grass, 'neath a blanket of dew,
that was cleared with the shovel, shiny and new,
by Grandpa and me on Tu B'Shevat.

This is the picnic we ate (wouldn't you?)
in the shade of the tree (and the tree's feathered crew)
that once was a sapling (from the small seed it grew!)
that drank up the water, splish-splashy and blue,
that moistened the soil, rich through and through,
that covered the seed with a green curlicue,
tucked into the peat, a warm, mulchy stew,
that lined the hole (but that you knew!)
that we dug in the grass, 'neath a blanket of dew,
that was cleared with the shovel, shiny and new,
by Grandpa and me on Tu B'Shevat.

This is the branch (what a great bird's-eye view!)
that reached over the picnic we ate (wouldn't you?)
in the shade of the tree (and the tree's feathered crew)
that once was a sapling (from the small seed it grew!)
that drank up the water, splish-splashy and blue,
that moistened the soil, rich through and through,
that covered the seed with a green curlicue,
tucked into the peat, a warm, mulchy stew,
that lined the hole (but that you knew!)
that we dug in the grass, 'neath a blanket of dew,
that was cleared with the shovel, shiny and new,
by Grandpa and me on Tu B'Shevat.

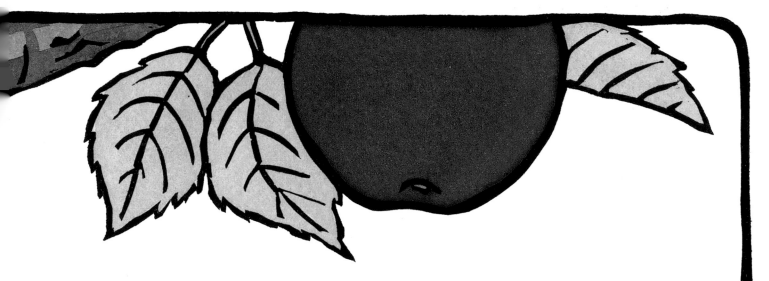

This is the fruit, which, right on cue,
grew on the branch (what a great bird's-eye view!)
that reached over the picnic we ate (wouldn't you?)
in the shade of the tree (and the tree's feathered crew)
that once was a sapling (from the small seed it grew!)
that drank up the water, splish-splashy and blue,
that moistened the soil, rich through and through,
that covered the seed with a green curlicue,
tucked into the peat, a warm, mulchy stew,
that lined the hole (but that you knew!)
that we dug in the grass, 'neath a blanket of dew,
that was cleared with the shovel, shiny and new,
by Grandpa and me on Tu B'Shevat.

This is the seed playing peek-a-boo,
that hid in the fruit, which, right on cue,
grew on the branch (what a great bird's-eye view!)
that reached over the picnic we ate (wouldn't you?)
in the shade of the tree (and the tree's feathered crew)
that once was a sapling (from the small seed it grew!)
that drank up the water, splish-splashy and blue,
that moistened the soil, rich through and through,
that covered the seed with a green curlicue,
tucked into the peat, a warm, mulchy stew,
that lined the hole (but that you knew!)
that we dug in the grass, 'neath a blanket of dew,
that was cleared with the shovel, shiny and new,
by Grandpa and me on Tu B'Shevat.

This is Grandpa's shovel, now rusty and worn,
that I use to dig a hole on a Tu B'Shevat morn'
to be certain this tiny new seed is sown—
just me and a grandchild of my own.

Ten Great Ways to Celebrate Tu B'Shevat

Tu B'Shevat (the 15th day of the Jewish month of Shevat) is sometimes called the New Year or Birthday of the Trees. Here are some ways you can join the celebration!

1. Invite friends to a fruit-and-nut-tasting party. Learn the *brachot* (blessings) to be said before eating each variety. Try an Israeli or traditional Jewish recipe using fruits and nuts.

2. Find out how other nations and cultures honor trees (such as the celebrations of Arbor Day in the United States, Shikmokil in Korea, and Chih Shu Chieh in China).

3. Learn about the work of the Jewish National Fund (JNF). Donate money to buy a JNF tree in honor or in memory of someone special.

4. Start an ecology or environmental club. Help save a rain forest. Weed a public garden.

5. Read a book about Johnny Appleseed.

6. Choreograph a dance, sing a song, draw a picture, or write a poem about trees.

7. Walk through the woods. How many different species of trees can you identify?

8. Find out what the Torah teaches us about the importance of trees.

9. Make a flowerpot out of recycled materials. Put a small, easy-to-care-for plant in it, and bring it to a resident of a nursing home.

10. Hug a tree. Better yet, plant one! To plant a tree like Grandpa's, visit your local nursery. Find out which species grow best where you live. Ask if the seeds for your tree need special care or preparation before they can be planted. The nursery will give you good directions for planting your seeds.

About the Author and Illustrator

Marji E. Gold-Vukson is a former elementary public and religious school teacher. She is the author of several books for Kar-Ben including *The Shapes of My Jewish Year* and *The Sounds of My Jewish Year*. She lives in West Lafayette, IN, with her husband and five children.

Leslie Evans has a BFA in printmaking from the Rhode Island School of Design. She has worked as a designer and freelance illustrator for many years. In addition to her art, Leslie enjoys printing books and broadsides at her letterpress studio in Massachusetts. She lives in Watertown, MA.